To Mark Cass, Geoff Gnaggs, and the other friends of my youth in Sherburn in Elmet, in the West Riding of Yorkshire

Brock
Anthony
McGowan

First published in 2013 in Great Britain by
Barrington Stoke Ltd
18 Walker Street, Edinburgh, EH3 7LP

www.barringtonstoke.co.uk

ISBN: 978-1-78112-208-2

Printed in China by Leo

One

The old male shifted in his sleep. He was fighting
again those long-ago battles, back in the days
when his teeth were still sharp. Those teeth
were worn down to brown stumps now, but once
every living creature feared them.

He remembered the big fox he had killed
in a clash over earthworms. Then there was
the mink, a cruel invader from other lands. It
had come down in search of his young. That
was a fight that he would not forget – the
deep puncture marks in his throat helped him
remember.

But before then, back when he was a kit, there was the time when men had come with dogs and they had killed and killed. Only he had got out, carried away in the mouth of his mother. She had put him in a safe place, and gone back for the rest of her litter. But she had never returned, and so he had been left alone in the wide world.

Somehow he had survived, with worms and fallen fruit for food. The first winter was hard, and he had frozen and he had starved. But he had endured.

And now here he was. The old king, asleep in his sett. Strong still, but fading.

But his memories scurried back to the men and the dogs, and all of a sudden his senses came awake.

The scent was strong. And now so were the sounds. He felt the fear run through the tunnels

and sleeping chambers, and he knew that the time had come.

He stretched himself.

Yes, there was still one last fight in those old bones.

Two

"Wake up, Nicky, wake up!"

I didn't want to wake up. I wanted to stay asleep. And even more than that, I wanted to stay in my bed where it was warm. Ever since the boiler bust the mornings had been hell. In the night your breath would freeze on the inside of the window so you could write your name in it with your fingernail.

"Wake up, Nicky, wake up. You've gotta come."

It was Kenny, of course. Kenny's my brother. People say he's simple, and he is. I know you're not meant to say 'simple-minded' any more, but

it seems to me that it's the exact right word for Kenny. He hasn't got all the stuff going on that messes up other people's heads. He isn't always trying to work out the angles, or how to stitch you up. He thinks other people are as kind as he is, and he only has one idea at a time.

His brain was starved of oxygen when he was getting born, so now he has what they call learning difficulties. But, like I say, I think 'simple' is better and kinder and truer than talking about 'difficulties' or 'disabilities'.

Sometimes I wish I was simple, and happy, like Kenny.

"C'mon, Nicky," Kenny pleaded.

I half opened an eye and checked the window. It was still as black as death outside.

That half-open eye was my first mistake.

"Ha!" said Kenny, and his voice crackled with joy. "I saw you. You're awake. C'mon, we've got to go."

"Get lost, Kenny," I said. "It's too early, and it's flipping freezing."

But it was no good. He yanked me out of bed, and before I knew what was happening I was pulling my kecks on.

"What the heck is this all about, Kenny?" I said. I was trying not to sound angry. You can't sound angry with Kenny or he gets upset.

"Just come on," he said. "It's good."

Three

"This better had be good," I said to Kenny when we were half way down Moorgate, the main street in the village. It was so cold outside it made your teeth ache, so you had to shut your mouth and breathe through your nose.

Calling Moorgate the main street makes it sound a bit too grand. There was a Spar, and two pubs – The Oddfellows Arms, where my dad goes, and The Red Bear, where he doesn't, cos he's barred. Then there's a hairdressers, and the closed-down social club, and that's about it.

At the traffic lights we went down Kirk Lane, which has the fish-and-chip shop on it, and

another pub called The Foresters, and at the end, the church.

It was light enough now to be able to see the top of the church against the sky. The church was really old and always looked spooky but somehow morning spooky wasn't as bad as evening spooky. It was as if you knew that all the ghosts and vampires and that sort of thing had already gone back to their graves and coffins or whatever.

If it had been later me and Kenny would have been trying to scare each other by going *wooooooooooo!* but now we just walked along thinking about how cold it was.

I was wearing my parka but I was still shivering like a junkie. Kenny was wearing his red bobble hat, but apart from that he just had his stupid Dr Who sweatshirt on, and his jeans, and I could see that his hands were blue.

I felt bad about that, and not just because the sweatshirt was the uncoolest item of clothing ever created. I should have made him put his coat on on top, but my head had been all foggy. Kenny never felt the cold at all until he was frozen solid, and then he'd howl and wail until you got him home by the gas fire.

Anyway, by now we were heading down the lane that goes between the fields, and I began to have an idea where we were going to end up.

Four

Most of the land around here is dead flat. Because it's so flat, almost every inch is planted over with fields of wheat and other stuff, I don't know, maybe beetroot or whatever. My dad tells me that there used to be hedges in between all the fields, and that you used to get skylarks and lapwings and loads of other birds. But now all the hedges have been dug up, and it's just the flat fields and the only birds are fat pigeons and scrawny rooks.

Like I said, it's almost all dead flat, but there's one place where the ground sort of folds in to make a 'V' shape, like a kind of mini valley.

Tractors and ploughs can't get in it, so they haven't bothered to chop down the scrubby little patch of trees that grows there. It's only about a hundred metres long and maybe ten metres wide, but it was the nearest thing we had to a spot of wilderness. Everyone called it the Copse, but I think it had some other name, a proper name, but nobody could remember it.

You'd sometimes hear an owl hooting in the dark depths of the Copse, and I once heard the drumming of a woodpecker. I never saw it, which is a shame, because I'd really like to see a woodpecker. I've always been into birds and animals. I had a notebook where I'd written all the birds I'd ever seen, but it wasn't that many because, like I say, round here it's not that great for birds.

I wish I still had that notebook. Our mum gave it to me before she went off. But Kenny scribbled all over it and then my dad threw it away.

Me and Kenny once built a den in the Copse.
That was when we had bikes, so it didn't take so
long to get there. But my bike got nicked, and
Kenny tried to customise his. He took it all to
bits and then, like Humpty Dumpty, he couldn't
put it back together again.

My dad would have mended it, but … well, he
had his troubles.

Without bikes it took just a bit too long to get
to the Copse, so we abandoned the den, but that
didn't matter because it was a shit den anyway.
Just some branches propped up against a fallen-
down tree, and it was full of earwigs and black
beetles.

"Are we off to the den, Kenny?" I asked. I
thought he'd maybe decided that we should fix it
up again.

"Yeah … No," he said back, which wasn't a lot
of use.

And then I heard a dog bark. It's funny how you can tell the size of a dog from its bark. Well, maybe not that funny. It would be more funny, I suppose, if you heard a little yap and it came from some big bugger the size of a pony. Or if there was a massive deep bark like a lion, and then you saw it had come out of a little mutt the size of a crusty snot.

But anyway, you could tell from this bark that it was a big dog. And I knew which big dog. And then another dog joined in, and another, and you didn't have to be Sherlock bloody Holmes to know what dogs they were and who we were going to meet.

I grabbed Kenny by the arm and made him face me.

"Kenny, what is this?" I demanded. "Tell me now."

But Kenny twisted away and started to lope off towards the Copse and the sound of barking.

His long arms and legs flapped and flailed about
like clothes on a washing line when the wind
blows.

"We gotta be there before it starts," he yelled
back at me, and then he fell over his feet. If I'd
reached him before he got up I'd have dragged
him home, but I didn't. I only caught up with him
when he was already in the trees and then it was
too late.

"Look who's here," said Jezbo. "It's Mental
Kenny and Nicky the Poof."

Five

There were three of them there. Well, six, really, if you counted the dogs. Rich and Rob Bishop were twins. They had long yellow hair and they looked a bit like angels, but it would be a big mistake to think they were angels, because they weren't.

Rich was mean. Even at junior school he used to punch kids and take their pocket money. And he was a dirty footballer. If you went past him or skilled him up, he'd just hack you down, even if a teacher was watching.

Rob wasn't mean. He was something else. He was a psycho. He'd seem all friendly and normal,

and then something would set him off and he'd smash stuff up. 'Stuff' could mean you, if you were around. He once bit a kid and the kid had to go to hospital to get a shot for tetanus and probably rabies as well. Rob was on Ritalin but it didn't make any difference.

In a way it was easy to get by with Rich, because at least you always knew what he was going to do. But Rob was like a firework that you think has gone out, and then you go back to it and it blows your head off.

The third kid was Jez Bowen, who everyone called Jezbo. Jezbo was 17 years old, which made him the leader of the rest. He was massive, and pretty thick. Two of the dogs were his, and one belonged to Rich.

Me and Kenny didn't have a dog because my dad said we couldn't afford it.

Jezbo's dogs were like Jezbo, but maybe a bit less thick. One was a pitbull crossed with

something bigger than a pitbull. Maybe a Rotty, or one of them other dogs with slavering mouths and flabby jowls. I hate dogs that drool on you while they bite you, because I think that's taking the piss.

That dog was called Satan. Kenny once called him Santa by mistake, and so sometimes the other kids would call him that too, but not when Jezbo was around.

Jezbo's other dog was just a normal pitbull, a bitch he called Slag.

Satan and Slag.

That told you all you needed to know about Jezbo.

Rich and Rob's dog was a Jack Russell terrier called Tina. It was an evil little scamp, but not that scary because it couldn't reach your arse to bite it even if it jumped.

Six

It took me a few seconds to work out what was happening.

The whole lot of them were standing around the base of a tree. I'm good on birds and animals, but I don't know much about trees so I can't tell you what kind, but it was big and old. It was growing out of the slope on the edge of the Copse. You could see its roots going in and out of the soil, like dolphins going in and out of the water.

There was a hole there in the earth between the roots. It was nearly big enough to get your head into.

That was the sort of thing Kenny would do –
stick his head into holes and get it stuck.

Rich and Rob had spades. Jezbo had a
hammer, for some reason. The dogs were going
mad, running around and sniffing and barking.

"What's going on, Jezbo?" I asked, but I
already had a sick feeling about it. I thought
maybe they had a fox trapped in the hole.

"Badger sett," Jezbo said. "Gonna play with
the badgers, isn't that right, Kenny?"

"Yeah!" Kenny said. He was grinning from
ear to ear.

So that was what this was about. Jezbo had
sent Kenny to get me to join in the fun. Well, I
didn't want anything to do with this.

"You don't need us here," I said. I didn't quite
look Jezbo in the face. I was thinking about the
hammer.

Jezbo had a smirk on his face you wanted to wipe off with a brick. "Kenny, you want to play with the badgers, don't you?" he said.

"Yeah!" said Kenny. "That's why I come. And I brung me brother, so he could play too, like you said."

"We have to go home, Kenny," I said, and I put my hand on his shoulder. "Let's go and get some breakfast. There's some Frosties in the cupboard."

Kenny jerked away from my hand like it was a hot iron.

"You always stop me playing," he whined. "I'm not going home. I'm not hungry. I don't like Frosties."

"Course you do," I said back, in a soft voice. "It's Weetabix you don't like. And scrambled eggs."

"You're both staying," said Jezbo.

"I'm not," I said. "This is wrong. It's against the law."

I knew it was a mistake as I said it. Rich and Rob copied my voice. "Against the law," they said, in a sarky way that made me sound like a big ponce, and they all whooped and jeered at me.

"Shame your dad never thought about that when he had all them knock-off DVDs in your shed," said Rich. Rob laughed and they both looked over at Jezbo. His smirk got even bigger, like a fat slug on his face.

Seven

I better explain about the DVDs, and why they all found it so funny.

My dad was on bail because the police found some DVDs in our shed. Jezbo's dad, Mick Bowen, had told my dad that they were pirate copies. He said that even if they got done for it, it was only copyright infringement, and no one got banged up for that. He offered my dad £200 to keep them for him, and my dad said yes. He didn't have much choice because Mick Bowen sort of ran our village, and you couldn't really say no to him without getting your windows smashed in and, maybe, your kids beaten up.

The trouble is that the DVDs weren't pirate copies at all. They were real ones, thieved from a warehouse down in Birmingham. So my dad was getting done for handling stolen goods, and he was looking at doing time inside. The police told him that if he grassed up the people who had dumped the DVDs on him, then he'd get off with community service. But my dad wasn't a grass.

Before all that happened, my dad was OK. He was never totally right after our mum left, but he kept trying. There was always food on the table, and we had OK clothes. He ran a fishing tackle shop for a couple of years. Then he sold crap – dishcloths and stuff like that – at the market in Pontefract. Then he delivered flyers and other junk mail round the village. He even had a paper round, for a while, but he stopped that when he heard that me and Kenny were getting teased for it by the other kids.

But after the thing with the DVDs, Dad
stopped fighting. He spent all day watching telly,
and then drank cheap supermarket lager in
the night. He didn't do anything bad. He didn't
do anything at all, really. I think he was just
waiting to find out what would happen. If he got
jailed, then we'd end up in care. I think he was so
scared about that that he could only cope with it
by blanking it out.

Anyway, that's what they were all sniggering
about in the Copse, and it's another reason I had
to hate Jezbo and his dad.

So, Jezbo came over to me and put his
massive arm around my shoulders. The dogs
came over, too. Jezbo's dogs, I mean. Tina the
Jack Russell was straining at its leash, trying to
get down the hole.

"I'm not gonna make you stay," Jezbo said.
"Free country and all that shit. But then poor old
Kenny will be all on his own, without his little

bwover to *pwotect* him. And them badgers can be savage …"

We both knew that Jezbo wasn't really talking about the badgers.

I shrugged. "I'll stay," I said. "But I don't want 'owt to do with this. It's not right."

"Please yourself, mummy's boy," Jezbo jeered. "Oh, I forgot. You haven't got a mummy, have you?"

Rich and Rob laughed at that, and as usual when anyone else laughed, Kenny laughed too.

Then Jezbo ignored me, and they got down to work, while I stood and watched like a dummy.

Eight

They'd already found two other holes further down the bank, and now they pegged nets over them. Kenny did most of the work, while the others yelled at him and told him what to do. Then they got ready to put Tina, the Jack Russell, down the main hole.

The thing is, I knew they were doing it all wrong. They were acting like they were ferreting for rabbits. You net the holes in a rabbit warren and put a ferret down, the rabbits shit themselves and bolt out, and then you've got them in the nets. I didn't know much about badgers, but I knew they weren't like rabbits.

"They'll kill that dog," I said.

I didn't mean to help them, but I didn't want to see Tina get killed. She was a little menace, but she wasn't deep-down bad like the other two dogs.

"Shut yer trap," Rob said, "or we'll stick you down the bloody hole."

They all had another good laugh, and then Rich put Tina into the hole. Like I said, she'd been straining at her leash until then. Now she had a quick bark and a sniff and came right back out again.

So, she wasn't *that* daft.

Rob said some bad words to her and grabbed her by the scruff and shoved her in again. She tried to come out, but Rob stuck his arm right into the hole to ram her back. And then Tina was off, her little legs scurrying into the blackness.

"This is gonna be good," said Jezbo. He had a big wet grin on his ugly face. "Get ready by them nets."

Rich and Rob went and stood by the side holes. They each had a sack. I suppose they planned to put the badgers in the sack when they ran out and got tangled up in the nets. I'd seen a dead badger on the road once, and it was massive. I wouldn't have fancied trying to wrestle it into a sack, even if it was caught in a net.

Nine

They were all laughing and joking to begin with, but then a noise came out of the hole. In fact it came out of all the holes. It seemed to come out of the ground itself and well up through the soil. First there was a growl, a dog's growl, then a sort of a hiss, I suppose, but not like a cat. It sounded like the sort of noise that would come out of a dragon or something like that. I mean something from a story, not real life.

And then came the mixed-up sound of a fight – snarls, growls, and yelps of agony.

"Go on, get stuck in, lass," Jezbo shouted into the main opening. It was almost sort of funny, I

mean talking into a hole like that. But it wasn't really funny, because you could imagine what was going on under the ground, and that was horrible.

It was even more horrible when the noise stopped, and then all there was was a giant silence, like in outer space.

"Shit," said Jezbo.

I don't think I've ever heard anything as quiet as that sound after the fighting stopped. It was like the whole world stopped with it. There was no sound of the wind, and not even the annoying squeaking of a sparrow. Even those two mad dogs Satan and Slag stopped barking.

Then Jezbo came out with a stream of bad words.

Rich and Rob came back from the side holes.

"Where's our Tina?" Rob asked.

"Shut up," said Jezbo.

That would normally be enough to set Rob-the-nutter off, but like everyone else he was afraid of Jezbo – afraid enough to keep his mad side under control. For now.

"We'll get a new dog," said Rich. "A decent dog. Tina was a stupid bitch."

That made Jezbo and Rob laugh, but I don't even know if Rich meant it as a joke.

Ten

"Right, let's dig these buggers out," said Jezbo. Then he pointed at Kenny. "You, get here."

"What for?" said Kenny. He had stopped grinning. Even he knew that something was wrong.

"Cos I said," Jezbo said. He thrust a spade into Kenny's hand. "Now start digging along there."

Like I said, the main tunnel went along the side of the bank, so all you had to do to open up the tunnel was to dig into the bank a bit.

Kenny wasn't much of a digger. He just sort of poked around, which drove Jezbo mad. He

shoved Kenny out of the way and called Rich and Rob over. The three of them got down to it, and we were sent off to mind the nets.

Jezbo was manic. He hacked away with his spade like crazy, opening up the tunnel with great scraping hacks. Rich and Rob got stuck in too. Rich had the other spade, and Rob used a big stick like a kind of pick. He jabbed at the soil, and his brother scooped it away. Soon they had about ten feet of the tunnel dug out.

I suppose I could have run off with Kenny while they were digging, but I knew Jezbo would come after us and get us in the end.

Plus there was something else.

Something in me wanted to see how this would end up.

I could see that there was a kind of insane energy in Jezbo. It was like he was possessed by a demon. And it was sick and it was wrong. But

it was also kind of magnetic. I couldn't have torn myself away even if I'd wanted to.

But there was one thing I could do.

I left Kenny by one of the holes and went to the other. As I pulled the net back with my foot, I glanced over to Jezbo and the others to make sure they weren't watching.

Then I stood back, and waited.

Eleven

Badgers aren't like rabbits. They won't just bolt out into a net that's waiting for them. They've got more brains than that.

Jezbo and the others were working their way along the bank. There weren't any side tunnels for them to worry about, so they were going quite fast. Soon they'd reach the badgers, and then it'd be a blood bath.

Then I saw a flash of black and white from the tunnel nearest me.

I don't know why badgers have black and white noses. It's rubbish camouflage – you see it straight away. Or maybe that's the point –

maybe badgers are such tough critters that the black and white is a sort of warning. 'Mess with me and I'll chew your face off' sort of thing.

Any time you see anything wild like that – I mean something wild that you don't see very often – it always takes your breath away. For a moment I forgot about Jezbo and his mates. In fact, I forgot about everything in the world except for me and this little black-and-white face.

I was as still as death, so as not to scare it back in. The nose came out into the light. Then flickered into the dark again.

"Any sign of them badgers at them holes?" came Jezbo's voice.

I looked up. Jezbo was staring at me. He looked like he suspected I was up to something.

I shrugged. "Nah. Maybe there's none down there."

"None down there? You stupid poof! What killed Tina then? Bloody worms?"

Rich and Rob laughed like jackals. You'd never guess Jezbo was talking about their own dog that they'd been playing with half an hour earlier.

There wasn't much I could say to that, so I said nothing. But Jezbo's joke seemed to have made him forget about me, cos then he asked Kenny if he'd seen anything. Kenny said no, and then Jezbo got back to digging.

I looked back at my hole. I was really worried that the noise might have scared the badger back down for good, and that would mean death. It would get dug out by Jezbo and then killed by those two big dogs. I didn't want that.

But no, the black and white nose was back again. But it was … *complicated*. There was something different. Then I realised there was something in its mouth. I couldn't tell what at first, and then I saw that it was another badger – a baby one!

The badger carrying the baby came running out of the hole at top speed. It was clear it was scared shitless. It – well, I suppose it was a 'her' cos it must have been the mum – was only about two metres from me. I could see the silver hair on her back.

She went off through the bracken and brambles and the crud on the ground. And then it got even more amazing. Another little badger followed her. And another. Three babies. Well, not tiny babies. They were about the size of a puppy. And then they were gone.

Safe, I thought.

There was a smile on my face I couldn't hide.

"What you grinning at?" a voice demanded.

Twelve

It was Rich this time. He started to walk over to me, with his spade in his hand. He was covered in muck and he looked like he wanted to kill something.

Or someone.

I moved next to the hole as fast as I could. As I squatted down, I put the net back over it.

"Think I saw something," I said, peering down into the blackness.

"Has he got one?" Jezbo yelled.

"Nah," said Rich. "He's seeing things."

Then Rich gave me the spade.

"You dig for a bit," he said, in an off-hand way that I found more scary than if he'd been yelling. He shoved the spade in my hand. "I'll watch the bloody holes."

I went and helped the others dig. I didn't mind now, as I thought all the badgers had escaped. In fact, I was so happy that I dug faster than Jezbo and Rob. There was something quite rewarding about hacking through the soil and opening the tunnel. You didn't half work up a sweat.

I didn't really mind that either. Everyone said I was too scrawny, and I thought the digging might help to build up my muscles so I looked less like a matchstick.

And then it all changed.

First we found Tina. I'd forgotten about her. She was jammed in the tunnel and almost bent in half. She was covered in bites and blood, and at first I thought she must be dead. But she

wasn't. She was still breathing. Jezbo reached in and dragged her out by the scruff. He threw her to one side like she was just some rubbish he'd found in there, a coke can or something.

I looked at Rich and Rob. Rich's face was blank, but you could see that there were mixed-up feelings going on inside. But in the end he chose to ignore Tina as well. She was left to shiver and tremble on the wet ground.

They dug on for a bit longer, and then it all really began to happen.

Satan and Slag had been lying there licking their arses and doing other bored dog stuff, but then Slag started growling. She leapt forward, with Satan right behind her. They both stuck their heads down into the hole, almost getting them jammed in there.

"That's more like it," said Jezbo. "We've got 'em now."

I stood back while Jezbo and Rob dug harder. Rich came back and grabbed the spade out of my hands, keen for a bit of the glory.

A minute later and the dogs went insane.

"There. I see him," Rob yelled.

I looked and saw that the tunnel had opened out. There was dried grass and leaves in there, but that wasn't all. Most of the space was filled up with a massive badger. I guessed he must be a real old boy – I don't know, a hundred or something in badger years.

As I watched, Jezbo hit the badger on the back with the flat of the spade. The badger sort of cowered down a bit when that happened, but then he grunted and spat and bit out at the spade.

"Hold them dogs back," Jezbo yelled. Rich and Rob grabbed one dog each by the collar.

I'll say this for the twins – they weren't cowards. The dogs were still going mental, and

they tried to bite at them to get loose, but Rich and Rob held them steady.

I saw Jezbo reach behind the old badger with the spade. Then he sort of shunted him out of the wider space, which I guess was where the old badger slept.

But then I thought that maybe the big space was the nest – if that's what you'd call it – where the mother looked after the young 'uns. And so maybe the old badger was guarding her. Or rather, making sure that no one came after her.

If he'd been left in his den with his back covered then I reckon that old badger could have taken on anything. A lion or a tiger, even. But now Jezbo had dragged him out on to the scrubby grass, where there was nothing to cover his back.

"Let 'em go," he said to Rich and Rob, and they released Satan and Slag.

Right up until then I think Kenny had thought we were just going to play with the badgers.

You know, pet them and stuff. So now, when the attack began, it took him a while to understand what was going on. For a couple of seconds he was grinning.

"Are the dogs playing with the badger?" he asked. He strained to see past the bodies in his way.

Then the savage snarls and screams of pain reached a level that even his innocent mind could understand. "Are they fighting?" he asked. "What are they fighting for? What's going on?"

And then he ran away into the trees, crying. I should have gone to him, but I couldn't drag myself away from what was happening on the grass.

Thirteen

There was something wrong with the badger's back legs. Maybe its spine was bust or something. I don't know if it had happened when Jezbo hit it with the spade, or if it was already crocked. Maybe that's why it didn't try to run off.

It didn't really matter now anyway. For whatever reason, it couldn't move too well. And it was under attack, with two massive, evil dogs snapping and chomping at it from every side. The badger would shuffle on its useless back legs to go for Satan, and Slag would dart in for a bite. Then the badger would go for Slag, and Satan would strike.

It was rotten to see, and I wished I could pull myself away.

But I was there now, until the end, and it made me feel dirty.

One thing that helped the badger was that the dogs couldn't seem to get a grip on its tough old hide. And when at last Slag managed to grasp it, it was a bad move. A bad move for the dog, I mean. The badger's skin was sort of loose, like a sock that's too big for your foot. So even with the dog's big teeth in the back of its neck, the badger could still sort of move inside its own skin and get its head around.

It seemed to be the moment the badger had been waiting for. He may have been old and slow, but those jaws of his hadn't lost their power. He opened them wide – much wider than you'd have thought was possible. In that instant I saw his teeth, and they were a mess – all broken and black. But there were a couple of long jagged

ones left, and now he fastened them around Slag's throat.

I think I knew at that moment that the big dog was as good as dead. There was something about the way the badger looked that made you think, 'OK, so you are never letting go, are you?'

It didn't matter that Satan was free now – not even this badger could bite two dogs at the same time. Satan sank his teeth into the badger's back, and at last he cut through the tough pelt and drew blood. He snapped and snarled and bit down and pulled and twisted and tossed, but the badger just ignored him.

The badger had a job to do.

A hard job.

A painful job.

A job that would kill him.

But he was going to do it.

The job was just to hold on.

Up to this point Jezbo, Rich and Rob had been laughing and yelling and cheering, like it was a football match or something.

"Kill him, Slag."

"Go on, 'ave him, Satan."

That sort of thing.

But now that changed. Jezbo tried to use his spade to free Slag from the jaws of the badger. But it was almost impossible while the three animals rolled and thrashed together. He kept trying to jab down with the sharp edge of the spade, but most of the time he just plain missed. Once he hit Satan a sharp blow on the head.

That was bad luck on Satan, but it got him out of the way for a second.

"Hold him!" Jezbo commanded, and Rich and Rob both grabbed the stunned dog.

The badger still had a death grip on Slag's throat, and the big dog's eyes were wide with terror and pain.

There was something else about them too –
you could see the light leaving them. They were
growing duller with each second that passed.

Now Jezbo could swing his spade. He lifted it
up over the two fighting animals and brought it
down.

I couldn't watch any longer. I turned away
and looked for Kenny. He was nowhere to be
seen.

Then I heard a sort of wail from behind me.
It was Rich, I think.

"What have you done?"

I turned back and saw what had happened.
Jezbo had missed the badger with the spade, and
struck his own dog. If it was in trouble before, it
was in *dead* trouble now.

Jezbo stood with the bloody spade in his hand
and looked at the still body of Slag. His face was
as blank and white as a rolled-out pizza base
before they put the toppings on it.

The badger had let go and was lying on its side. It looked half dead itself. Then Jezbo let out a scream and started to hit it with the spade, over and over again.

That's when I went home. I ran all the way, half blind from the tears I was crying.

Fourteen

When I got home I went up to Kenny's room. When he was a kid and he got upset he always used to hide under his bed. He was there now.

"Come out, Kenny," I said.

"I don't want to. I don't like what they did."

"They're not nice people, them, Kenny," I told him. "You won't play with them again, will you?"

"No."

"Come out and you can have a Mars Bar."

That got him out. It always did.

"Where is it?" he asked.

"I'll go to the shops and get it later."

Kenny looked cheated, as well he might. But then his face changed.

"Did they kill that badger?" he asked.

I nodded. And then I told him about how I'd let the mum badger and the babies escape. That made Kenny clap his hands and laugh.

"I lost my hat," he said. "My red one that our mum gave me. It must have fell off in the trees."

"I'll get it for you later," I said, "when I go to buy your Mars Bar."

That's why I was back in the Copse a couple of hours later. I found Kenny's hat right away. You couldn't miss the red in all that green and brown. Then I went back to where we'd dug the badgers out. The old badger was still there.

He looked even bigger dead than he'd looked alive. He was as long as both my arms, stretched out. It didn't seem right to just leave him there. I was scared to pick him up – I thought he might have fleas or something – so I used my foot to

shove him over to his den. It was hard work, and it felt wrong – kicking an animal when it was down, sort of thing. But I got him there, and then I covered him over with the loose soil that was scattered around.

It was a rubbish grave, but it was better than nothing. I even thought about saying a prayer, but then I felt stupid. So I just said 'sorry', you know, for the part I played in killing him.

There was no sign of Slag. Jezbo must have carried her off. But I did find Tina. She was lying in the same spot where she'd been left. I thought she must be dead, like Slag and the badger. But she wasn't. She'd always been a feisty little menace, but now she lay as gentle as a lamb and just looked up at me. I cursed Rich and Rob, then, for leaving the poor little dog here to die alone.

I picked her up.

"There, there," I said.

I put my fingers near her mouth and she licked them. I decided then that I was going to give her to Kenny to look after. If Rich and Rob complained, then I'd point out they'd left her for dead, so they'd given up any right to her. And if they said any more about it, then I'd fight them.

I should have gone home then but for no good reason I decided to have a look at the holes we'd netted up. And there, in the one I'd let the mum escape out of, I saw something. First I thought it was a rabbit because it had a grey back. But then I got closer and I saw the little black-and-white face.

It was a baby badger.

There must have been four, not three, and this one got left behind. It was caught in the net, tangled up. It must have been struggling for ages, and now it was tired out.

I put Tina down and I began to unravel the badger from the net. I was worried it would try

to bite me, but it just lay there and let me free it. Either it was too tired to fight, or it was too small to have learned to hate humans yet.

I got it free and held it in my hands. It was about the size of the guinea pig we used to have at junior school – what was its name? Snuffy. Yeah, that's right, Snuffy.

I looked around. Was the mother about? Surely she would have come back before now, if she was coming.

I had my big coat on. It used to belong to my dad and it looked like something a tramp would wrap up in to sleep. I put the little badger in the pocket, picked up Tina, and went home.

Fifteen

There weren't any knock-off DVDs in the shed in our back garden any more, but it was still full of crap. There was a broken lawnmower, tins of dried-up paint, cardboard boxes full of wires for electrical gadgets that we didn't have any more, a broken spade, a broken plant pot and a broken radio.

I put Tina in one cardboard box, and the badger in another. Then I went to get Kenny.

My dad was in the kitchen drinking something out of a chipped mug and reading a newspaper he must have found somewhere. He

needed a shave. Or to grow a proper beard. One or the other.

He looked up at me.

"Where have you been?"

"Just out."

"Bit early. Not up to bother are you?"

"No, Dad. Where's Kenny?"

Dad nodded towards the living room. I went in. Kenny was watching cartoons on telly. His eyes were bright with happiness. That was the great thing about Kenny. Terrible stuff could have happened ten minutes ago, but he'd forget it and just enjoy what was in front of his face.

"Kenny, come on," I said.

"Where? Have you got me my Mars Bar?"

Drat. I'd forgotten about the Mars Bar.

"I've got something better than that," I told him. "But we have to do something first."

And so I made Kenny stand outside the shed while I passed him out some of the junk in there.

Then we took it down to the skip outside number 54 down the road. As it was Saturday there were no workmen there to bollock us for it.

Then I let Kenny into the shed and showed him Tina. She managed to look up at him, and she gave her skinny tail a wag.

"Is that Tina?" Kenny said. His face shone with wonder. "I thought she was dead. Do we have to give her back to Rich?"

"No," I said. "They haven't got any right to a dog. I saved her, and I'm giving her to you to look after."

Kenny started to shout out his happiness, but I told him to keep quiet. He was literally shaking with excitement.

"There's something else," I said.

Then I showed him the box with the badger.

Kenny let out a great sigh.

"*Aaaaaaaaahhhhhhhhhhh!* Is it ours? Can we keep it? What's its name?"

I thought of the school guinea pig. "Snuffy," I said. "And it's a massive secret. If Jezbo finds out, he'll kill him for sure."

"I don't think Dad will let us keep it," Kenny said. For once he'd hit on the truth of things.

"Well let's make sure he doesn't find out," I said.

"But can I tell him about Tina?" Kenny asked. "He used to have a puppy, he told me. But it ran away after the milk van and never came back. He'll let me keep Tina. It's not like Snuffy."

I thought for a couple of seconds. I didn't see how we could keep the little dog a secret forever. Plus I reckoned she needed fixing up a bit, and my dad was always good with us when we got bashed or cut up as little kids. He could get out a splinter before you'd even felt it. 'Look out of the window,' he'd say, and then when you looked back it would be gone.

"Yeah," I said. "You can tell Dad. In fact why not show him now? But remember, not a word about Snuffy. If he asks, Tina got in a fight with another dog."

So Kenny picked up the box with Tina in it and took it to Dad, who was still in the kitchen reading his paper. Only he wasn't really reading it. He was just staring into the space where the paper happened to be.

"What you got there, lad?" he asked, when Kenny put the cardboard box on the table.

"It's my new dog," said Kenny. "She's called Tina. She got bitten by Santa."

Dad looked at Kenny, and I thought he was going to smile, which he hadn't done in a long time. But then he looked back at the dog, and there was nothing there to make anyone smile.

"I found her in the Copse," I said.

"Been in a bit of bother, girl?" said Dad. He peered at Tina. "Let's see what we can do for you."

Then he picked Tina out of the box and put her on the newspaper he'd been reading.

"Go and get me the TCP from the bathroom," he said to me. But Kenny ran off and got it. He came back with nearly everything from the bathroom, including toothpaste and shampoo. But the TCP was there. It must have been bought when Mum was still here. Lucky it's not the kind of thing that goes off.

Dad filled up a bowl with warm water from the kettle, then poured the TCP in it.

"Get us some bog roll," he said.

Even Kenny couldn't mess that one up.

Sixteen

Half an hour later, Tina was looking a lot better. She was still limp and floppy, but the cuts were clean, and her eyes were brighter.

"We should take her to the vets to get her stitched up," my dad said. "But ..."

He didn't need to finish. There was no money for the vet.

"We'll take care of her, Dad," said Kenny.

My dad nodded at him. Somehow, in the time it took him to clean up Tina, the whole question of us being allowed to keep the dog had been forgotten.

"Aye, well," Dad said. "See that you do."

I looked at the kitchen clock, which was stupid as it hadn't worked for two years. It only needed a new battery, but that sort of thing never got done in our house. The clock on the cooker still worked. It said it was only eleven in the morning. It felt like too much had happened for it still to be the morning.

"I'm off out," my dad said.

Dad had looked different when he was working on the dog – more like I remembered him. But as he got up and walked out of the house, that all went again. His shoulders slumped like he had a heavy shopping bag in each hand.

"Give Kenny his dinner," he said, without looking round. "And his tea."

"What is there?" I asked.

"I dunno. Beans on toast."

The kitchen door swung behind him, but didn't close properly.

The rest of that day was all right. We needed money for dog food, so me and Kenny scraped together what was in my sock drawer and his piggy bank. We had seven quid.

"You stay here and look after Tina," I said. I went down to the Spar and bought two tins of cheap dog meat.

When I came back the house was empty. I got in a panic and ran out to the shed, not sure what I was going to find. Well, actually I had a good idea what I'd find, I just didn't know how it would pan out.

Kenny looked up, with a gummy, goofy smile.

"They're friends now, Snuffy and Tina."

Kenny had put Tina into the cardboard box with the little badger. I don't know if it was because Rich had drowned all her puppies not that long before, or if it was just that she was still too sick to move away, but Tina had curled herself around Snuffy. The badger had its head

resting on her side, and its little black eyes looked up at me.

"Do you think they'll get married?" Kenny asked.

I laughed.

"No, it's more like Tina's his mum," I told him. "I can't believe it. You'd have thought they'd hate each other. What happened when you first put them in together?"

"Well, Tina sort of scrunched up in the corner like she was scared. But then Snuffy went up to her and said hello in badger talk, and then they were best friends."

I put my arm around my brother.

"You're *my* best friend," I said.

"Get off!" he laughed, embarrassed. "You're my second best friend, after Samit. Samit can do the sound of a machine gun and he can burp the whole alphabet."

"So can I," I said. But I only got as far 'g' before I lost it, and started laughing.

I went back to the kitchen, opened the dog food and put it on two plates, then brought it back out. I lifted Tina from the box and put her on the floor next to one plate, and I put the other in the box with the badger. Kenny watched all this without blinking, like he was watching one of his cartoons.

Tina ate all her food up straight away, and then looked up at me, wanting more. The badger was a bit slower, but then he began to nibble. He ate half of what I'd given him, and I gave the rest to Tina. Then the badger did a wee and a poo in the box, which made Kenny laugh like mad. He kept saying 'badger poo, badger poo' over and over.

"Take Tina out into the garden," I said to him. "I bet she needs to go to the toilet, too."

Cardboard boxes were one thing we had plenty of, so I chucked the dirty one away and got a fresh one. This time I put a load of torn up newspaper in the bottom.

Kenny appeared at the shed door. "Tina did a wee. But she didn't want to do a poo."

"OK, Kenny."

I looked at Tina. She was still pretty shaky, which is what you'd expect after the morning she'd had. I was going to say we should bring her back in to the house with us, but then something made me pick her up and put her back with Snuffy. The two of them curled around each other again, as if they'd spent their whole lives doing it.

We left them to snooze.

Seventeen

I had to scrape some blue off the bread before
I could make Kenny's beans on toast, but I read
somewhere that it doesn't do you any harm.
Then I told Kenny to go and play at Samit's
house. Samit's mum and dad are dead nice.
Samit is a couple of years younger than Kenny,
so they can play together OK.

   Then I went down to the library. The library
used to be open all the time, and I used to like
going there when my mum and dad fell out. Also
it's good sometimes to have somewhere to go
that's free.

The library lady has big hair and glasses on a chain round her neck, just like you'd expect, but she's always dead nice to me. She saw that I liked books about space and aliens, and sometimes she used to recommend things to me, but most of the time, she just left me to get on with it. I don't know what her name is, which is why I always just call her the library lady. She's got a name badge, but it's small and I don't want to stare at her chest in case she thinks I'm a weirdo.

Since the cuts, the library's only open some of the time. But on Saturday afternoons it's open until 2, so I was OK.

I looked in the big reference books first, but there wasn't much about badgers. I mean, there was loads about their skeletons and that sort of thing, but nothing about how you'd take care of one. Then I went and asked the library lady if there were any books on badgers. She looked on

the catalogue on her computer. "I thought so ..." she said.

The book was just called *Badger* and it had everything you could want to know about badgers in it. It was one of the books you're not allowed to take home, but I didn't mind. I sat down at one of the big wooden tables and spent an hour going through it. After that I felt like I was an international badger expert. I knew what they ate (worms), where they lived, what sort of sounds they made, how big their families were, loads of stuff like that. But I still didn't know how you'd look after one.

But one thing did stick in my head. The book said that most times there was a main sett where the badger family would live. There'd be quite a few badgers there of different ages, and there'd be loads and loads of tunnels and entrances.

But then you'd also get what were called 'outliers', which were small badger setts with just one main tunnel. Sometimes a couple of badgers from the main sett would move into an outlier for a while, and then go back to the main sett.

That made me think that the sett that Jezbo had destroyed must be an outlier, and the main sett would be somewhere else. And then I began to think that maybe we could find the real sett, the main one, I mean, and take Snuffy back. Could you do that? Would the mum have him back after I'd touched him and passed on my human smell? It didn't say in the book.

"Did you find out what you needed to know?" the library lady asked when I put the book back on the shelf.

"Yeah, sort of. Not everything."

"Is it for your homework?"

I nodded. I hated to lie to the library lady, but I couldn't tell anyone that I had a badger,

could I? Lying with a nod didn't seem like proper lying, cos it didn't come out of my mouth.

"Why not look online?" she said. "You'll probably find there's lots more information there."

It wasn't like the library lady to tell you to look stuff up on the internet. She always said the internet was full of rubbish, and that books told you the truth. Plus there was normally a wait to use the two crappy computers they had there, while other people tried to find jobs or sell their junk on eBay. But for a change there was nobody using them, so I went and had a look for badger stuff.

There were a couple of good websites, and at last I found out what I should be feeding the badger on – the dog food was fine in fact, as he was too old for milk. But what I really needed to know wasn't there. But one of the sites had a contact phone number. I wrote it down on a

scrap of paper, said thanks to the library lady, and ran home.

Eighteen

I checked on Tina and the badger. The badger
was licking at Tina's cuts. I felt weird inside. For
the past couple of years all my softness had been
saved for Kenny. The rest of the time, I'd made
myself hard. I mean hard as in not feeling stuff,
not thinking about stuff, not caring about stuff. I
could never be hard like Jezbo or Rich and Rob.
I didn't even want to be. Anyway, I hadn't felt
much about anything for a long time. But now
I stood and looked at those two little creatures
in that scuzzy old box and it made me feel ...
something.

Then I remembered that I hadn't given them any water, so I went to the kitchen and filled up a bowl. When I put it in the box they untangled themselves and slurped it all up together. I filled it again, and left them to it.

I had a phone call to make.

"Hello, Badger Trust."

The guy who picked up the phone didn't sound like the friendliest man on the planet. Plus he came across as a bit bored. Straight away everything I'd meant to say went out of my head.

"Er, hello."

"Can I help you?"

He sounded even more annoyed now. I suppose it was because I was a kid.

"Yeah, I've, er, got this badger."

"It's alive?"

"Yeah, course. What would I want with a dead badger?"

"Is it injured?"

"No. It's a baby. Not a little baby. I mean a – "

"You know it's illegal, don't you, to take badgers from the wild?"

"I didn't take it. I found it. It was on its own, it's mum had gone off."

"How do you know? Mothers will sometimes leave the young if you disturb them, and then come back later. Was it near the sett?"

He didn't sound bored any more.

"Yeah, no, sort of," I said. This badger bloke had got me sounding like Kenny.

"What do you mean?"

"Well, it was near the sett, but it had been … er … they couldn't use it any more."

I could *feel* the man thinking. I'm pretty sure that he knew what had gone on. I don't mean *everything* that had gone on – I mean the basics. I mean that the badgers had been dug out and baited.

"*Where are you, son? Can you tell me your exact location?*"

There was a threat in his voice now.

"I've just got a question, that's all."

"*I can trace this call, you know. I can find out where you are. You could be in serious trouble.*"

That was a mistake. He shouldn't have threatened me. Definitely shouldn't have bluffed me.

"You're the bloody Badger Protection League, not the F-B-bloody-I," I said. "You can't trace anything. I've got a simple question. I want to help this badger. Will you help me do it?"

I heard the man take a deep breath to get a grip on himself.

"*What is it you want to know?*"

"The sett where I found him ... it got smashed in. But it was a – " I tried to remember the name. What was it? "Out, out something ..."

"*Outlier?*"

"That's it, an outlier. There was just one tunnel. So I think there must be the main sett somewhere near."

"Possible, yes, possible."

"And my question is, if I find it, will the other badgers take the baby back again?"

There was a pause. The man didn't make any noise, but I could tell that he wasn't angry or bored any more. Now he was trying to work out what the best thing to do was.

"Yes, most time they will," he said. *"The sooner you get it back, the better. But, look, if you tell me where you are, we have volunteers all over the country who can take this over. And if there's been any criminal activity around the badgers then, as long as you played no part in it then you won't get into any serious trouble."*

I thought about me and Kenny helping to dig out the sett. I thought about what Jezbo and Rich

and Rob would say. I knew we'd end up getting the blame, some of it at least.

But I thought about something else as well. Me and Kenny had had a bad few years. Nothing much good had happened to us. And for that matter we hadn't done much good, either. But with the badger there was a chance for us to make a little difference to the world. We could put some goodness in, like sugar in tea.

"Thanks, mister," I said. "I'll send you a postcard."

It wasn't much of a funny comeback, but funny comebacks weren't really my thing.

I was about to slam the phone down when the man said, *"My name's Steve. What's yours?"*

And I said 'Nicky', without really thinking. But then I did think and I knew it didn't matter because there are millions of kids called Nicky in the world, and I could be any of them.

Then I did put the phone down.

By now it was five o'clock and I was knackered – I'd been up since before dawn, remember. I went and lay on the couch in the living room. The telly had been on all day, with the sound turned off. Kenny liked it like that. He got a bit freaked if he ever came in and the telly was off.

I closed my eyes for a second. When I opened them again I knew that a lot more than a second had gone by, and that something was wrong.

Nineteen

I rushed out to the shed. The door was open. There were voices from inside.

"This one is the badger," one was saying. "He's called Snuffy, and he's mine. You can't pet him because if he bites you he'll never let go. Then they'll have to take you to hospital in the ambulance and have Snuffy cut off by a doctor."

"Kenny," I said from the door, "you promised that you wouldn't tell Samit."

They both spun round. Samit was holding Tina. The eyes behind his thick glasses were as big as dinner plates.

"No I didn't!" Kenny said. I don't know if he meant that he hadn't promised or that he hadn't told. I loved Kenny, but he could be a massive liar.

"I won't tell anyone else," Samit said. He held the dog close to him, as if he thought that would stop me from getting mad and whacking him.

"If you do tell anyone, Jezbo will find out and he'll come and kill Snuffy," I said. I was trying my best to look and sound scary.

It worked, but only because Samit was 8 years old. If he'd been 9, he'd have seen through me.

Samit and Kenny both looked down at their feet.

"OK," they said.

"You can feed them their dinner," I said, a bit softer.

"OK!" they said again in totally different voices.

I heard my dad come in late. Kenny was asleep. The animals were out in the shed.

I thought my dad was going to be drunk, but he wasn't. He looked tired.

"Where you been, Dad?" I asked.

"Looking for work, son."

He hadn't tried to get work for ages.

"Any luck?"

He shrugged. "There's nothing happening around here. Might as well look for work at the North Pole."

Even though he looked tired, like I said, there was something a bit different about Dad tonight. He didn't look happy, but he looked a tiny bit less sad than normal. I mean that thing he said about the North Pole – it was almost a joke. I couldn't remember the last time he had tried to make a joke.

I wanted to ask him about it, but I didn't know how to put it into words. So I made us each a cup of tea and waited for him to tell me.

"I was in town," he began. Then he stopped and blew across his tea to cool it. I sat across from him at the kitchen table and sipped my tea. The table top was covered in scratches and marks. I saw where Kenny had written 'Keny' with the point of his fork.

"I went into Starbucks," Dad said. "I had a voucher for a free coffee that I tore out of the newspaper. There was someone there I used to know from school. Don't look so bloody startled. Aye, I went to school too, you know. She went off to become a nurse. She works at Seacroft now. We got talking, and she said they need care assistants on the ward."

"Care assistants?" I said. "What's that?"

"Just someone who helps the nurses," Dad said. "Changing bandages, wiping arses, getting

the patients fed, that sort of thing. She said that I'd got more exams than most of the people that work there. She reckons they'd take me on for training, if she put a word in for me."

"Did you tell her about the … trouble, the trouble with the police and that?"

My dad nodded.

"She said it would be OK as long as I didn't get a prison sentence. You know, as long as it was just community service."

I knew my dad was trying to tell me something. It wasn't just that he had a girlfriend. Or might have a girlfriend. And maybe even a job. There was something else as well. But he didn't tell me then, not with words. We sat and finished our tea without saying anything else, but you know how some silences are filled with tension and make you feel sick?

Well, it wasn't one of those.

Twenty

Two things woke me up the next morning. The first was the sun coming through the window. The curtain had fallen down yonks ago, and I didn't know how to fix it. It didn't matter much when it was dull or rainy outside, as it was most days, but when the sun shone it got me right in the eye.

The second was the noise. It was a bit like the sound of the sea in a seashell, and a bit like the sound of birds in the morning. But it wasn't the sea and it wasn't birds.

I got up and went outside just wearing my pyjama bottoms.

A crowd of little kids was bubbling around
the door of the shed, like the froth when you
shake a coke bottle.

I should have been mad. But I just couldn't
be. Not when I saw the way that Kenny was
lording it over them. He was a sort of king, or a
god, even, because he had the magic thing in his
arms, the wild thing.

Yeah, the stupid berk was holding the little
badger out to show them all, and they were
taking it in turns to stroke it. What gave it all an
extra edge of drama was that the badger would
have a little snap at the fingers that tried to
touch it, which made the kids squeal out in fear
and joy.

"Bloody hell, Kenny," I said. I tried to get a bit
of the badger's bite into my voice. "What are you
playing at?"

Kenny wasn't listening. Maybe he couldn't
even hear. There must have been fifteen kids

there. They were crammed in the shed, like Quality Street when you first open the tin at Christmas.

"SHUT UP!!!" I yelled, and they did simmer down. I shoved my way to the front. It was like wading into the sea at Bridlington, with the waves slapping at your thighs.

Samit was holding Kenny's piggy bank. Tina had her paws up on the rim of the box so she could watch everything. She looked OK, in spite of the scabs she had all over her from the bites.

As I watched, another kid put 10p in the piggy bank and tried to stroke the badger.

"That's enough, Kenny," I said.

"Why?" Kenny asked. "I've nearly filled my piggy bank up again. We can get chips or anything. I said to Samit I'd buy him some if he held the piggy bank."

"Kenny, have you got the faintest flipping idea what a secret even is?" I said. "Who told them about this?"

"Er, it was sort of my fault, Nicky," Samit said. He looked a bit sheepish. "I told my brother, and then he blabbed."

"I don't blame *you*, Samit," I said. "I told Kenny not to tell anyone. As soon as one person knows this sort of thing, everyone knows it. Especially in a place like this. If the police find out, or ..."

"If the police find out what?"

Well, that got rid of the little kids. They scattered like leaves in a gale, revealing the tall, gaunt figure of my dad in the shed doorway.

Twenty-One

My dad said 'oh' when he realised what Kenny was holding.

No – actually he didn't say 'oh'. It was just that his mouth made the shape it would have made if he had said 'oh', but nothing came out. The first words he actually said were 'Bloody hell!'

Kenny stared at my dad, then at the badger, then at me. Then he thrust the badger behind his back.

"I haven't got anything," he said. "Have I, Samit?"

Samit looked around in confusion. My dad
helped him out.

"Go home, Samit lad," he said. He didn't say
it unkindly.

Now all the other kids had melted away
and it was just me and Dad and Kenny and the
badger. Tina was still looking over the rim of her
box.

"Where's this from?" my dad asked.

"I don't know," said Kenny. He'd stopped
trying to hide the badger and was holding it in
front of him again. It didn't seem to mind.

I thought I'd be best off with the truth. So I
told Dad about Jezbo and Rich and Rob, and the
death of the old badger.

When I said Jezbo's name my dad stiffened,
like someone had yanked the hairs at the back
of his neck. But he didn't say anything until
I'd finished the story. About half way through

Kenny got bored with holding the badger and put it back in the box with the dog.

At the end my dad said, "You can't keep it, son. There's laws about this. If the police find out I've got a wild animal, I'll be in breach of my bail. You know what that means."

"I know," I said. "But I've got a plan."

I thought my dad was going to ask me what the plan was, but he just said, "It's gone by next weekend. At the latest."

Twenty-Two

I'd always been a bit of a loner at school. There were a couple of kids I sometimes used to hang out with at break, but that was it. And I'd join in if there was a big footie match on in the playground. I didn't get picked first or last – I was one of those kids in the middle, not so good or so crap for anyone to care much if I was on their side or not.

But most of the time it was just me, sitting on a bench reading a book or walking around trying to stay out of trouble.

I used to quite like it when it rained, because then I could spend break in the library. If you

got there early enough you could even get on the computers.

It was raining today. And that was good, cos I had work to do.

I knew from the badger book I'd read that there would be a main sett within a couple of miles of the outlier in the Copse. And I had a rough idea what I had to look for. The book said that badger setts are nearly always on the edge of a wood, right next to fields. Badgers like to be able to forage in the woods for worms and beetles and that sort of thing, and then go and eat whatever's growing in the fields. Sweetcorn, carrots, whatever.

So I got straight onto Google Maps and started searching. I put in our postcode and zoomed and scrolled around until I found the right place.

Even just on the normal view it was amazing.

Like I said before, all I'd ever seen when I looked at the countryside were the bare fields. But that was wrong. I'd lived there all my life but all of a sudden now I could see loads of things that I never even knew were there. There were little streams and, more importantly, woods. Some of them were quite big. The thing is that a lot of them were miles off the main roads, so you'd never know about them. I thought I might have spotted some of them from the top deck of the bus, but not in a way that had sunk in.

When I switched to the satellite view it was even better. You could zoom right down so you could see every single tree.

I'd always thought about the place I lived as a bit of a dump. But now I saw it like this, from above, with the fields and the trees, it looked like a nice place after all.

By then the break was over and I had to go back to lessons. It didn't matter. I'd found what I

was looking for. Just a mile away from the Copse there was a small wood.

And Google Maps even gave it a name.

Brock Wood.

And because I'd never heard the word 'Brock' before I looked it up. That's when I got really excited.

Brock was an old word for badger.

Twenty-Three

After school I asked my dad if he'd help me fix up Kenny's bike. Dad had been filling out some forms on the kitchen table. I couldn't remember the last time I'd seen him doing that sort of thing. I thought it might be something to do with the DVDs and the court case.

"That bike's a bit small for you," he said.

"I know, Dad, but it's the best I've got and I need it for ..."

"For this plan of yours?"

I nodded.

He sighed and put down his biro. "I'll get my tools."

Even when Kenny's bike was new it wasn't a cool one. It wasn't a mountain bike or a racer or anything like that. It was just a kid's bike, maybe for a nine year old. And now it was a mess, with brown paint flaking off and rust all over it, like dirty dandruff. Both tyres were flat. We pumped one up OK, but the other had a puncture. My dad fixed it, then fitted the wheel back on. He fixed the breaks and then he looked at the gears.

"I can't fix them," he said. "But I can lock it in second gear for you, so it won't be too bad."

It took about an hour, and at the end of it I had a rubbish, uncool bike. But it was a rubbish, uncool bike that I could ride.

Kenny had appeared from school half way through. For once he didn't gabble away. He just stood and watched Dad work. I don't think he could remember seeing Dad do anything like this before.

"Can I go on it now?" he asked when it was finished.

"I'm just gonna test it for you first," I said.

I was off before he had the time to come back at me.

To get to Brock Wood, I had to bike down the lane past the Copse. The bike was fine as long as the going was flat or downhill, but going up even a little hill was torture. The bike was old and it was small. I prayed nobody saw me, cos I must have looked pretty stupid.

After the Copse there were more fields. Some had sheep in, some were empty. Then there was a railway line with a tunnel under it. We never used to come this far when on a walk. Every step was double, as you'd have to come back again the same way.

I hadn't printed off the map, as you had to pay 20p a sheet at the library, but I remembered it really well. There was a sort of a track just

before the railway line. It was too rough to cycle on, so I wheeled the bike. The ground rose up a little – more of a hump than a hill. Then there it was. Brock Wood.

On Google Maps it had looked dead small, but now I was facing it, it seemed like a forest. How had we never discovered this before?

I knew one thing – it was too big for me to explore in one evening. It was already starting to get dark. At least I knew what I was looking for. Big holes, on the side of a bank, or in the roots of a tree. They should look like a capital 'D' lying on its side.

There was a barbed wire fence between the wood and the field. I held up the top strand but I still managed to snag my hoody as I ducked under.

I knew I only had a few minutes, so I focused on the part of the wood right where I came in. It was beautiful under there. The trees were much

taller and fatter and more ... I don't know what the best word is ... majestic, yeah, much more majestic than the trees in the Copse. And it all just felt older, as if there had never been a time when this wood didn't exist.

I broke a stick off a hazel bush and used it to swipe and swish my way through the undergrowth, like an explorer with a machete. I found rabbit shit, birds' nests and an old pram someone had dumped a hundred years ago. Then I found the remains of some tramp's campfire and a hole that might have belonged to a mouse or a rat. Or maybe it was just a general hole that didn't belong to anything.

I even found a long axe-handle, broken off near where the axe-head would have gone. It was smooth and heavy, and I wanted to keep it. But I knew it'd be tricky to cycle with it, so I stuck it in the ground near one of the barbed

wire fence posts. I thought I could collect it one of these days.

So, I found lots of cool stuff, but I didn't find the badger sett. It didn't matter, I told myself. I had all week.

Twenty-Four

The next day was Tuesday. I dashed back from school as fast as I could, and spent two hours looking for the sett. I searched along the next part of the wood, where it met the field.

Nothing. Well, nothing except for nettle stings and bramble scratches all over my arms.

When I got home Kenny and Samit and a couple of the little kids were in the shed playing with Tina and the badger. It looked like the badger craze had cooled down a bit.

Tina was looking much better, more her old self. Only the old Tina would have chewed your

face off rather than let someone kiss her the way
Kenny was doing.

Wednesday was a copy of Tuesday.

I was starting to worry. I'd just assumed
that the sett would be somewhere near the edge
of the wood. But what if it wasn't? If it was
somewhere deep in the wood then it could take
weeks and weeks to find it. Or I might never
find it. But I had to. Everything depended on me
finding that badger sett and giving Snuffy back
to his mum.

Up till then I hadn't told Kenny about Brock
Wood. I didn't think there was any point in
putting stuff in his head that might fall out again.
And if it fell out, who knew who might pick it up
again?

But now I reckoned I needed him.

So on Thursday I told Kenny to borrow
Samit's bike, and we cycled down the lane
together.

The trip had a bit of a funny side, as Kenny wanted to go on his own bike. So I had to ride on Samit's, which was even smaller than the one my dad had fixed up. We must have looked like a couple of clowns.

But it was also ... I don't know ... *special*. We hadn't done this sort of thing for a long time, and it felt good. It felt free. All of the bad things that were in my mind, the bad memories, the regrets, the pain, they all got blown away by the wind and by Kenny's laughter.

Anyway, we got there and started searching. Kenny thrashed away with a stick through the nettles and pretended he was killing demons or orcs or I don't know what.

With Kenny doing the hard work, I decided to try to use my brain, to think like a badger. I'd read in the badger book that they needed dry soil, so I didn't bother looking anywhere where the ground was soggy. That helped, as a muddy

stream ran through the wood, and a lot of the ground was quite damp. Then I looked for spoil, which is what they call the earth the badgers chuck out of the sett.

After an hour we'd found nothing. Kenny had given up by then, and he was climbing trees. He was a good climber. But he was an even better faller, so I thought I'd better get him and go home. We still had one more day to search, and I didn't really fancy carrying Kenny home with a broken leg.

He was up in a big old tree with knotted bark and branches that began quite low down, which is why Kenny had gone up it. I looked at the leaves, and even I knew it was an oak tree.

"Get down Kenny," I said. "We'll try again tomorrow."

"I can see forever up here," Kenny shouted back. "I can see the church and the chip shop. Can we get some chips?"

"Yes, Kenny," I said, "but not if you stay in that bloody tree. Now get down."

As Kenny started to climb down I kicked at some loose grass at the base of the tree.

Loose, dry grass.

Something else I remembered from the book. Badgers would often clear out the bedding material from their setts. That way they got rid of a few fleas and other vermin at the same time.

I felt my senses go into hyper-drive. I looked around for what had to be the opening of the sett. And there, in the roots of the tree, I found the hole. I don't know how I'd missed it up till now, but I had.

Kenny dropped down next to me, and did a forward roll. He'd seen someone do that on the telly once, a paratrooper or something, and so he always did it when he jumped.

"I've found it, Kenny," I said.

"I knew you would," Kenny replied. "You can do anything."

I don't know what Kenny really meant by that, but it made me feel warm inside.

"There'll be more holes," I said. "Help me find them."

We searched around and found two more openings. One was quite close, and the other was further away, under another tree.

"Job done," I said to Kenny, as we walked back for the bikes. "On Saturday morning we'll take Snuffy back to his mum."

"I bet she'll be glad to see him," Kenny said. When I looked at him I expected to see him grinning his grin, but he looked sad.

Probably just sorry about losing the badger, I thought.

Twenty-Five

My dad had a talk with me on Friday after tea, while Kenny and Samit and Tina had a last play with the badger. I told them that they shouldn't because he had to get ready to go back to his own kind. But they didn't listen to me, and I didn't have the heart to stop them.

As usual, my dad had a cup of tea to help him talk to me. In fact, he'd been drinking a lot of tea in the last few days. And not so much of the cheapo supermarket lager. Maybe we were so skint now that he couldn't even afford that?

"You know, Nicholas," Dad said, "that I might have to ... go away."

"Get sent down, Dad, you mean," I said. "Yeah, I know."

"And if I am, you'll be put into care, you and Kenny," he said.

I nodded.

"Well," my dad went on, "I've decided that I can't let that happen."

"There's nothing you can do about it, Dad."

"There is. There's one thing I can do."

It only took me a second to realise what he was saying. He meant he was going to grass up Jezbo's dad, Mick Bowen.

"You can't do that, Dad," I said. "Mick'll kill you."

"He won't kill me. They'll put him away."

"But what about when he gets out?"

My dad shrugged. "Me and Mick used to be mates, you know, back when we were nippers. Back then we both thought we'd end up underground, like our dads. But then the pit

closed, and there was nothing much for us. He went his way and I went mine. But he was never a ... a ... an evil man, Mick. Not like that son of his ... anyway, all I'm saying is that I'll do what I can to keep this family together."

I didn't know what to do then. I suppose I should have hugged him or something, but we weren't really a hugging family.

"What's happening with your nurse?" I said, after an awkward silence.

My dad did an embarrassed little laugh.

"Aye, well, I'm maybe seeing her tonight in the pub. She said she'd be in there. And I said I might be as well."

"Have you got a shirt ironed, and some clean kecks?" I asked.

And then my dad did a proper laugh.

"When I need you to tell me how to look smart, then that's the day I'll give up for good," he said.

And then he stopped laughing and looked at me, and what I was wearing. It was a mix of stuff that was too small, because I'd grown out of it, and too big, because it was his old gear that I hadn't grown into yet.

"There's not been a lot of cash around for new clothes, I know," he said. "But it's gonna change, son, for all of us."

"OK, Dad," I said. Then I went out to play with Kenny and Samit, so my dad didn't get even more embarrassed about me seeing him cry.

Twenty-Six

"Wake up, Nicky, wake up!"

It wasn't that early – it was light outside, but it was still cold, and I wanted some more time in bed.

"Go away, Kenny," I said. "We can take Snuffy down to the wood later. There's no mad rush."

"There is a mad rush," said Kenny. He was still shaking me. "He's not there, Nicky. And nor is Tina. They've taken them. Jezbo ..."

I was up in a second. I pulled on my jeans and t-shirt as I hopped across the bedroom floor.

Outside, the shed door had been kicked in. That was stupid. It didn't even have a lock. It just used to get stuck, sometimes. But it was a sure sign that it was Jezbo's work.

"Get Dad," I told Kenny. "Tell him to come to the wood past the Copse. It's called the Brock Wood – he might know that. Tell him to come as fast as he can."

"What are you gonna do?"

But I was already on Kenny's bike, and cycling as fast as I could.

I don't know how I knew where they'd be, but I knew it as sure as I'd ever known anything. I threw the bike down on the lane and ran along the railway line until it hit the woods. I could have done it with my eyes closed by now. But I didn't need to know it like the back of my hand today. I had something else to lead me there. The sound of dogs.

I didn't bother trying to crawl through the barbed wire fence. I just jumped it like an Olympic hurdler.

I hoped they wouldn't have been able to find the sett, but I suppose it's easy with dogs. There they were, gathered round the hole at the base of the oak tree.

There was Jezbo, of course, and Rich and Rob. And Satan, looking more evil than ever as he barked and drooled like a monster from a computer game. Last, I saw Tina. When she saw me she tried to come, but Rich had her on a tight leash, and he pulled her back with a savage jerk.

Snuffy was on the ground just in front of the hole. There was a piece of string tied to his back leg, so tight I could see it digging in. The other end of the string was tied to a tent peg they'd driven into the earth.

If Jezbo was surprised to see me, he didn't show it.

"Here he is, the poof who steals dogs."

"I didn't steal that dog," I spat back. "You left her for dead."

"Well," said Rich, "she's fine now. You looked after her nice for us. Lucky for you, otherwise I'd have to kick the shit out of you."

Rob laughed. Jezbo just stared me out.

I couldn't resist asking how they knew to come here.

"What?" Jezbo jeered. "After a spaz and a poof on baby bikes came out here ...? Did you think no one would notice?"

"I want my badger back," I said. I tried to hold Jezbo's gaze, but I could feel my guts turning to jelly.

"You can have it when it's dead," said Jezbo. "Him and his mam and his dad and the whole lot of 'em. They killed my Slag, and now they're all gonna die."

"And how do you plan on doing that?" I asked. And then it twigged.

I made myself laugh. "You lot really are thick, aren't you?" I said. "You're trying to lure them out with that badger there." I pointed at Snuffy. "Do you really think the others are gonna come out, with your stink in the woods, and that dog yelping and barking?"

"Aye, why not?" said Rob. "They'll come out when they get a sniff of him. We can wait. And when they come out, we'll do 'em."

Even as he spoke you could see the doubt begin to show in his eyes. So Jezbo took over.

"Dunt matter," he said, with a smirk. "If they don't come out, then we'll have some fun with this little 'un here. Then we'll dig the rest out, if it takes all day."

"No you won't," I said, and I clenched my fists. That made them all laugh again.

Jezbo stopped laughing and looked at me. All of a sudden he wasn't like a kid at all. He was something older and darker and more coldly evil.

"Look at where you are, poof," he said. "Go on, look around. There's no one here. We could do what we want to you. No one would ever know. We could kill you here. Cut you up. Feed you to the dogs."

And when he said it, with Rich and his psycho brother watching, I knew that they could.

So that's when I ran.

At first I heard a belch of laughter. One of them yelled out 'chicken' and another shouted 'run, you poof'.

But then Jezbo said, "Get him, don't let him go."

They thought I was running because I was afraid. And they were right. I was afraid. But I wasn't running away.

I reached the place by the fence where I'd stashed the axe handle. Rob was right behind me. He must have thought that I was stopping to climb through the fence. But I wasn't. In one movement, I pulled the handle out of the ground, turned and swung it so it hit Rob just below the knees. He was off balance, and the handle was smooth and heavy and hard as iron, and he was down.

I ran the ten metres back to the oak tree before the other two had grasped what was happening. They looked stupid with surprise when I burst back through the trees. I stood in between them and my badger and the opening of the sett.

Somehow Tina had slipped out of her collar, and she was by my side now, snarling at the others.

Rob came limping back, his face red with fury.

Now the three of them stood facing me.
Satan the dog was straining at the lead in Jezbo's
hand.

"Any of you come any closer, and I'll brain
you," I said, and I waved the axe handle in front
of me. It was a good weapon. I felt a bit like one
of the Knights of the Round Table, or something
like that. I also felt terrified. I couldn't fight
them all. I couldn't even have fought one of
them. But that wasn't what I was trying to do. I
was playing for time.

I thought that Rich or Rob or Jezbo would
come and have a go at me, and I thought maybe
I could get a couple of good hits in with the stick
before they got me. But I noticed that none of
them looked at me. They were all staring at the
thick smooth wood in my hand. I saw that they
were cowards, and that gave me a moment of
hope.

Then Jezbo unhooked the lead from Satan's collar. He was on me in a second. I only just had time to lift up the handle so that the dog's teeth closed around it rather than my face.

But the weight of Satan was too much to hold, and I fell back onto the earth. I heard Tina yap and snap at Satan's flanks, but the big dog just ignored her. His face was in my face, breathing the stink of old meat and blood over me. I made some sort of a noise – a wail or a squeal, I don't know. It was answered by the hysterical hyena laughing of Jezbo, Rich and Rob.

I closed my eyes and waited for the horror, for the teeth to tear at my cheeks, my nose, my mouth.

And then, somehow, the weight of the dog was off me. I opened my eyes, and saw my dad. He had hold of Satan's collar, and had lifted the dog into the air with one hand. The dog weighed as much as I did, or more, but my dad lifted him

like he was baby. He went over to Jezbo and took
the lead off him. Jezbo just stood there with his
mouth open. My dad fastened the lead to Satan's
collar, and then tied it to the stump of tree.

The dog shivered and whimpered, half afraid
of my dad's strength, and half strangled.

Dad came over to me and helped me up off
the ground. Then he turned to face the three
lads. His face was iron. His voice was iron
grating on iron.

"You set a dog on my boy," he said. "You
were here to kill badgers. If you were men I'd
make you pay for this myself. But you're not
men, you're boys, and you're up to your scrawny
necks in it."

"Shut up you dosser," said Jezbo, getting his
voice back at last. "You're nothing but a loser
and a tramp. And you'll do whatever my dad
says, just like when you had them knock-off DVDs
in your shed. You're so thick you believed him

when he said they weren't robbed. And now you're too chicken to grass him up, cos you know what he'll do. And – "

But that was as far as he got, because at that moment a massive fat figure came pushing through the bushes, puffing and panting. He was followed by a much thinner one.

"That's interesting," the fat man said. "Backs up some other stuff we've been hearing."

"Snuffy! Tina! You're OK. I've come to save you!"

The fat man was the village copper. His name was Jim Shepherd, but he was called Shep by everyone. Shep was a drunk, and a lazy sod, and he never solved any crimes that anyone could remember. But he was here now.

The other person was, of course, Kenny, who came running up to us, not knowing who to hug. Tina jumped up into his arms and solved the dilemma.

I looked at my dad. "What ...?"

"I went round to the station, when Kenny told me what was up. Shep drove us here. Sorry it took so long."

"It's all right Dad. You got here, thanks to Kenny." I put my arm around Kenny, and Dad hugged us both.

Ten minutes later me and Dad and Kenny and Tina were alone there on the edge of Brock Wood. Shep had led the others away, all now as scared and sulky as Satan.

My dad undid the string around the badger's leg. It turned to lick at the sore place where the string had dug in.

"Snuffy's looking at us," said Kenny. "He's saying goodbye."

And that is what it looked like, sort of. Then the little badger trotted towards the opening under the tree. I'm not sure, but I thought I saw

a flash of black and white snout welcome him home.

Twenty-Seven

It was six months later, at the end of summer.
The past week had been dead hot, but at five in
the morning it was quite chilly, and I wished I'd
worn my jumper. We were crouching down a few
metres away from the badger sett in Brock Wood.
There was me, and Kenny, of course, and my dad.

And my dad's girlfriend, Jenny.

Jenny was pretty nice. She was good at
calming Kenny down when he got upset. And
cos she was a nurse she was brilliant when he
fell out of trees and stuff and got bashed up, as
he often did. And she'd given me a PS3 she'd got
cheap on eBay.

My dad had pleaded guilty to handling
stolen goods, and he got away with fifty hours
of community service. He was going to have to
give evidence against Mick Bowen, but the police
had loads of other stuff on him, so Dad's evidence
wasn't that important. Bowen sent a message to
my dad just saying 'fair enough'.

Jezbo and Rich and Rob got community
service, too, for the badgers and for setting the
dog on me. They sometimes gave me the eye if I
saw them in the village, and Jezbo used to draw
his finger across his neck, like he was going to
slit my throat. But I knew it was just bullshit,
and that he was a coward.

My dad got the job as a care assistant. The
money was rubbish, but he loved it.

It was his idea that we walk here and try and
get a look at the badgers. I said there was no
way they'd come out if we were there, but Kenny
had picked up on it, and after that there was no

pulling out. I was surprised that Jenny wanted to do it, but she was quite good at surprising you. Maybe I just wasn't used to having a lady about the place. It was something we all had to get used to. Two ladies, I mean – Tina was our dog now, or rather Kenny's. He loved that dog more than he loved me and Dad, I think, and the dog loved him back.

My dad had scattered some of Tina's dog biscuits in front of the sett, but we'd been here half an hour now, and there was no sign of life.

I was about to ask if we could go home when I sensed Kenny going stiff, and he grabbed my arm.

"Snuffy!" he said in a whisper.

And there, in the shadow of the sett opening, was the distinctive pattern of black and white. The nose emerged, sniffed, and then went back in again, the promise of the dog biscuits balanced by the threat of the dog. We all breathed again,

having held our breath for those few seconds, and we got ready to go.

And then, all of a sudden a shape darted from the hole. It came towards us, and touched noses with Tina. Tina wagged her tail and did a little jump in the air. For two magical minutes the dog and the badger rolled and played together in the leaf litter. And then it was over. Snuffy took a biscuit with him and was gone, and we walked back through the trees and over the fields, home.

Our books are tested
for children and young people by
children and young people.

Thanks to everyone who consulted on
a manuscript for their time and effort in
helping us to make our books better
for our readers.

Acknowledgments

My thanks to the entire amazing team
at Barrington Stoke, but particularly the
wonderful Mairi Kidd, who badgered and
baited this book into existence.